The Story of Lippy the Lion

By Joanne Green
Illustrated by Marla Verdone

ISBN: 1-894936-67-1 Complete 9781894936675
Copyright © 2006Joanne Greene
SAGA BOOKS
Sagabooks.net

This book is dedicated to:
Jacob, Joey and Jessica.
They are my inspiration and my joy! ~ JG
To my daughters Lara Rose and Lexandra Ranae ~ MV

PERFECT BEAUTY

The Great Sphinx of Egypt has, over the years,
Lost her nose.
Venus de Milo has no arms,
And the Liberty Bell sports a great, wide crack.
And yet each of these is considered to be a thing of
beauty,
A standard of perfection.

And so it must be that we do not,
as one might imagine,
Look to perfection in order to see beauty,
But rather, we look to beauty,
And thereby see perfection.

It was a warm summer day when,
throughout the jungle,
there was a gentle stir.
The wind whispered to the mountains,
and the mountains nudged the trees.
The trees bent to tell the rivers
and the rivers carried the news
throughout the land.
A NEW PRINCE IS BORN!
Lippy the Lion was born!

Oh, how proud and happy his mommy and daddy were – the King and the Queen of the jungle. And yet, with their happiness, there was some worry. You see, handsome and strong as Lippy was, there was also something different. And that something different worried Mommy and Daddy Lion very much. Lippy's mouth looked a bit unfinished.

Lippy had a "Cleft Lip". It didn't close up right when he was being made inside Mommy Lion. When he was born, his lip really looked like it was broken. Mommy and Daddy Lion didn't know what to think. But when their baby lion looked up at them and grinned his big, wide grin, they knew that their baby was something wonderful and special. If only they could help his lip to grow together like other lions' lips! Mommy Lion held her son close to her heart. "Oh my darling baby," she said, "I would do anything, ANYTHING at all, to take this away!"

Very soon, the Jungle Doctor came to Mommy and Daddy Lion with a plan.

"We can help Lippy," he said. "But it might take some time to get it all right again."

Lippy's mommy and daddy wanted to do whatever they could to make Lippy's mouth work like every other lion's mouth.

And so, they asked the Jungle Doctor to help Lippy.

First, Mommy Lion was given a special bottle so she could feed Lippy, and so that he could grow bigger and stronger right away.

The Jungle Doctor wanted to do an operation that would help Lippy's lip to grow together and to look and work a lot more like other lions' lips look and work.

Mommy Lion was afraid. An operation is a scary thing when you are a Mommy Lion and the operation is for your baby! She did not want Lippy to have to hurt, and she was afraid for him. But she also wanted Lippy to be able to eat and talk like every other little Lion. She wanted Lippy to make friends and she wanted all the other Lions in the jungle to see just how handsome Lippy was. But she was afraid that the operation would hurt him.

Mommy Lion worried and fretted over the operation idea and she finally decided, "NO! My baby does not have to go through an operation just to be loved! I will have Daddy Lion proclaim throughout the jungle that everybody will accept Lippy like we do, even with his different lip." She went to Daddy Lion with the idea.

Daddy Lion looked sad. "I love our beautiful son too, my Dear, JUST THE WAY HE IS, but you must understand. I cannot proclaim for the whole jungle to love him as we do. I cannot tell all the animals to look past what they do not understand. I love his big wide smile, and I will miss it when it is gone, but I cannot order all the other animals in the kingdom to love it as well."

Mommy Lion was not happy with her husband's reply. She spoke with the Jungle Doctor again. "My Lippy is just fine," she said. "It is the rest of the jungle that is wrong. They will not accept my baby as he is because his lip is different, and I do not want to change his beautiful face!"

The Jungle doctor looked at Mommy Lion with concern in his eyes. "So, you do not want to fix what does not work?" he asked. "You do not want good health for your son?"

"Of course, I want him to be healthy," said Mommy Lion.

"Then he must have an operation to fix what does not work," said the Jungle Doctor. "Sure, the Hyenas might laugh and the monkeys might tease, and the animals of the jungle could very well turn from him when they see him. And perhaps you can pass a law that they will not be so mean. But even if a law is passed to love your son as you do, his lip will still not work. I do not know much about laws or about making other animals keep them, but I do know about lips. I know that unless Lippy has an operation to fix his lip, he will have a very hard time eating. And later, he will have a very hard time talking. This is something that Lippy needs, and YOU, Mrs. Lion, need to let him have that operation."

The Jungle doctor took Mommy Lion to the river where the water was calm and still. "Look," said the Jungle Doctor, "and try to remember when you first saw Lippy, that day in the mommy-hospital when Lippy was born."

Mommy Lion looked into the water, and an image appeared. In the image, she was lying on the birthing bed, just like she did on the day Lippy was born. How odd that she would forget so much about that day so quickly! There was a bustle all around her, and suddenly, all became quiet. She heard the mewing of a newborn cub, but none of the birthing animals were saying anything at all. "My baby," gasped the image of Mommy Lion. "Is it a girl cub, or a boy cub?"

The birthing doctor looked up, and with a sad voice, he said, "It is a boy cub. There is a problem."

Fear raced through Mommy Lion's mind. "PROBLEM??? With MY baby? What problem?" she asked. Daddy Lion was by her side and she gripped his paw.

"His lip is different," said Daddy Lion.

"It is a cleft," the birthing doctor told her. "It can be fixed."

When baby Lippy was laid on Mommy Lion's tummy, she looked lovingly at him and stroked his soft baby fur. She looked up at Daddy Lion. "Oh my darling baby," she said, "I would do anything, ANYTHING at all, to take this away!" and then she cried deeply from her heart while Daddy Lion cried with her and the cub mewed quietly in her arms.

"Do you remember that moment?" asked the Jungle Doctor.

"Yes, yes, I do," cried Mommy Lion. "I remember saying that I would do anything to take this away."

"Well," the Jungle Doctor said kindly, "This operation is the 'anything' you can do."

Days later, Mommy Lion took her handsome son to the Jungle hospital and gave him tearfully over to the Operating Nurse. As the big doors to the Jungle OR closed, Mommy Lion cried and cried. Daddy Lion was there to comfort her, but the time seemed to stand still while Lippy stayed in the Operating room with the Jungle Doctor.

Finally, the big doors opened again and the Jungle Doctor came out. "Lippy is fine," he said. "You can see him now."

Mommy Lion rushed in to see her cub. She was amazed. His lip was fixed and there was no more cleft. He would no longer struggle to do the things that others did so easily, like talk and eat. There would not have to be a proclamation made to order the other animals to like her son. His lip had no cleft. Now, he would have nothing more than a small scar.

She held her little cub in her arms and very
gently kissed the stitches over his operation.
Oh, how she missed his big, wide smile. Oh,
how she missed his first face! And yet,
something in her heart stirred and then roared.
This new face was handsome too!

What she did for Lippy was right and good, and at last, Mommy Lion could see that. As the sun went down in the jungle that night, Mommy and Daddy Lion held their handsome cub and felt thankful. First, they were thankful for their wonderful cub. And then, they were thankful for the wisdom and skill of the jungle doctor who could make Lippy's lip whole.

On that day, the wind whispered to the mountains, and the mountains nudged the trees. The trees bent to tell the rivers and the rivers carried the news throughout the land. Lippy the Lion is FINE!

THE END

DURING SURGERY

Dear Doctor,

Please remember
That little face you are
Reconstructing is more than
Muscle and Tissue and Bone.
It is the smile that fills
My heart with joy and
Swells my chest with pride
And brings life and meaning
Into my every day.

And when it is you and him
Behind the Big Doors,
And me in the little room,
Waiting,
Please remember
You are working with more
Than just a life.
You have in your hands
A reason for living
As well.

And as you look upon your
Little patient,
A mere few pounds of person,
Remember that he is cherished,
And not by me alone,
But by the many
Whose lives have been touched
And enriched by his.

And, Doctor,
I will also remember
That I have chosen to trust you,
And to trust your skills,
And that by choice
I have entrusted his face
And his life
Into your skilled hands

But for these next few hours,
While you and he
Hide behind the Big Doors,
And I wait in the little room,
I hope you don't mind
If I also choose
To pray.

An appendix of support

For parents and families

Following are documents that can be found on the Wide Smiles website www.widesmiles.org.

They are presented here to help new families of cleft-affected children to understand and cope with the new situations in their lives.

First, it is important to say that while it is not wonderful when our children are born with a cleft, it remains nonetheless true that children born with cleft are wonderful.

I invite you to visit the Wide Smiles website for more information specific to your issues.

****** CLEFT FACTS ******

Below I have listed some Cleft Facts that you might find interesting. Some dispel myths, others are simply facts we should all be aware of.

Fathers, as well as mothers, can pass on genes that cause clefting.

Some clefts are caused by environmental factors, which means it didn't come from Dad or mom.

One child in 33 is born with some sort of birth defect.

One in 700 is born with a cleft-related birth defect.

Most cleft-affected babies are boys, however, it is not uncommon for a girl to be born with a cleft.

If a person (male or female) is born with a cleft, the chances of that person having a child with a cleft, given no other obvious factor, rises to seven in one hundred.

Some clefts are related to identifiable syndromes. Of those, some are autosomal dominant. A person with an autosomal dominant gene has a 50% probability of passing the gene to an offspring.

Many clefts run in families, even though there does not seem to be any identifiable syndrome present.

Clefting seems to be at least in part related to ethnicity, occurring most often among Asians, Latinos and Native Americans (1:500), next most often among persons of European ethnicity (1:700) and least often among persons of African ethnicity (1:1,000).

A cleft condition is determined during the 4th to the 8th week of pregnancy. After that critical period, nothing the mother does can cause a cleft, and nothing a mother does can avoid the cleft. Sometimes it is determined even before the mother is aware that she is pregnant.

A cleft is nobody's fault.

Lost and Found

Nine months is a long time to wait. It's especially long when what you are waiting for is your heart's desire. But nature dictates that we have to wait. And so we spend the long waiting months by dreaming and preparing for the child that is to be.

Meanwhile we have the hopeful assurance that all is going to turn out well. We visit our Ob-Gyn and he listens and pokes and measures and smiles. He tells us that all is "progressing well". We watch the fuzzy pictures of a living child on the monitor of the sonogram and hope to learn if it's a "he" or a "she". But the lively little lump squirming on the screen assures us that all is indeed well. We watch our bellies bloat and we feel the thumpings of life within. We rub the bump where the head should be and tell ourselves that all is well. And even though occasional doubts pester us, we know that everything is as it should be. All mothers-to-be worry, don't they?

While we waited we prepared. We prepared a bassinet with soft colors and muted tones. We pictured our sweet baby's head resting gently on the pillow. We collected a layette, fingering each little piece, smelling each new scent. Our baby would be so beautiful - so loved. We stood in the empty, waiting nursery, arms caressing the bump of our own flesh that itself caressed our baby, and we waited.

Fantasy plays a major role in preparation. We cannot prepare for any event unless we can fantasize that event happening. Fantasizing our baby was easy. We talked about our baby to every important person in our lives, and even some who were not so important. We tried out dozens of names until we found the one that perfectly suited the child we imagined ourselves to have. We sat in our rocker and imagined ourselves holding a bundle of pure treasure and singing sweet lullabies to hasten a peaceful sleep. We communed with our babies in fantasy long before our babies could accept that communion. We pictured our babies in our arms. We pictured them big and healthy one day, small and vulnerable the next. We pictured heads full of hair, and we pictured heads of soft down. We saw a boy, and then we saw a girl. But we never saw a cleft. That is, not until the morning she was delivered.

Suddenly the picture of that imagined baby was shattered. She was gone. The pink little face that we gazed upon so lovingly in our fantasy was marred by an open hole where the perfect rosebud lips should be.

The delivery did not go as we had imagined it would. There were hushed tones in the delivery room. The baby was rushed passed us. Something was said about a birth defect. But this was not the way it was planned. Our husbands and we were gong to share this experience. It was going to be so beautiful. But it's confusing. And what did they say about a birth defect?

When we saw our baby for the first time we weren't prepared. We had never seen a cleft before. What were those feelings we felt? They were so mixed. We asked ourselves, "Is this what they mean by a 'face only a mother could love'?" And we have to admit that there were times right at first that we wondered if even a mother could love that face.

Our culture dictates that there has to be an instant, magical bond that forms between mother and child. Why wasn't it there? What would all this mean? Could we even breastfeed our child? Will she live? If she does live, how could that "thing" be repaired? Why, oh why, had this happened to us?

Were there feelings you felt that you could not admit to, even to your own mother? Did you feel cheated? Ashamed? Angry? Unable to love even your own child? We don't feel them all, but we would not be normal if we didn't feel some of them. What we felt was grief. We lost the fantasy child. In its place was a child we never imagined. It's not the same as losing the boy we envisioned when "he" turned out to be a "she". Suddenly pink becomes the most beautiful color in the world. But we lost the "normal" child we assumed we would have. And in its place we have a child that we do not fully understand.

How can you grieve the loss of something you never had, or someone who never really existed? Simply. You did have it in your heart. She did exist to you. That normal, healthy baby was as real to you as anyone else in your life. You not only now must grieve the passing of that child, you must somehow deal with the concept that she was never real to begin with. It is more than a loss. It is almost a retroactive loss. You not only lost her - you never had her in the first place. There is an emptiness left that can only be described as a hole. And the child in your arms may not fill that hole right away.

Grief takes many forms. At first you may want to deny it all. Denial is funny. It is like anesthetized reality. With the help of denial you can look squarely at something difficult and not be hurt by it. You may wake up and think you dreamed it all. Or you may tell yourself (facts to the contrary - but that never dissuades denial) that it will somehow "go away" all by itself. You can deny that it makes any difference. You may hold tightly to your child and confront the world, daring anyone to even suggest that you feel anything but love for the child with the deformity (and still, in the recesses of your heart you wonder if you will ever be found out.)

Denial gives way to anger. You may feel angry at the doctor for having done something wrong, or for not having warned you of every possible inevitability. Or you may just be angry at the doctor for the way he handled the delivery. You may be angry at your husband, After all, it must have come from his side! Why hadn't he told you that he carried defective genes? Or you may simply feel that your husband doesn't feel the way you think he should feel - not sorry enough, not loving enough, not sensitive enough to what you are feeling. You may be angry with the baby. After all, there is only one thing you asked of your child - to be born healthy. And she wasn't. As ridiculous as your anger may seem, it's there. You are even angry at yourself.

Anger turned inward becomes guilt. Grief causes you to feel guilty. You wonder what you did during your pregnancy that could have caused this. Your mind wanders to every tiny indiscretion. A friend smoked in front of you once. You drank coffee in the early days of your pregnancy. You took medicine for your morning sickness. Whether or not your self-blame is groundless (and it usually is), you feel somehow that that is what made the difference, and you are to blame. You may blame yourself for thinking bad thoughts, or for watching a horror film during pregnancy, as though it somehow "marked" your baby. Or you may have remembered some particular sin in your past that has come back to haunt you, and your child's deformity is somehow God's punishment for the awful thing you did. Or you may search your childhood to think of anything you may have done that could have damaged your chromosomes. At any rate, you try to shoulder the guilt. After all, you were entrusted with the task of carrying this child. And somehow you did it all wrong.

Guilt leads to shame. You begin to find it difficult to talk to others about your child's condition without becoming defensive. You sense that everyone else in your life is disappointed in you for producing a less-than-normal child and you wonder how you will make it up to them.

Denial, Anger, Guilt, Shame. These are not the feelings of motherhood, are they? Actually, yes, they are. They are the feelings of grief, and from time to time every mother experiences some form of grief. But for you it came early, while you were defining your role as a mother. It may help to realize that you grieve because you love. If it meant little to you, you would never have grieved the loss of it.

But grief leads finally to resolution. One day you are holding your child and gazing into her sleeping face, and you realize that this is the little face you love. At that point you become ready to put aside that which was lost so you might fully embrace that which you now have found - the child in your arms. You learn that you have grown to love your baby as she is, not as you had hoped her to be. And you know that your love for her is as strong as any love shared between mother and child could be.

You do not love her in spite of the deformity, or aside from the deformity. You love her as she is. You will deal with the deformity. You find strength born of the love that you share with your child that helps you to deal with all that is necessary to insure her of a normal future. You find yourself able to look at your child's face and see a child, not a cleft. Your child ceases to be defined by her deformity any longer. You have reached resolution.

It is okay to grieve. In fact, it is necessary to grieve. The loss is real, even though what was lost was only imagined. It is only by grieving that you can eventually let go. It

is only by letting go of what is lost that you can embrace that which was found. Grief can take only minutes or hours, or it can take months. If you find it difficult to move through the various stages of grief, go to a counselor. You are only experiencing a temporary problem and you may need help to get over it.

In most cases, the stages of grief will return from time to time - even years afterward. As long as your grief does not interfere with your relationship with your child or your ability to be an effective parent it is normal. If that is affected, help is available. Speak to your craniofacial team or medical professional. You are as much their concern as your child is.

On the day your child was born, something was lost, and something was found. Concentrate on that which you have.

And congratulations. You have a beautiful baby.

THE IMPORTANCE OF A

MULTI-DISCIPLINARY APPROACH

Cleft lip and palate is the most frequently occurring craniofacial anomaly. Problems associated with cleft lip and palate can be adequately addressed in today's medical environment. However, because a child with a cleft represents a complex mix of problems associated with the anomalyy, a team of professionals most effectively approaches the reconstruction process.

Treatment of a cleft begins at birth and continues throughout the child's growing years. While different needs are more pressing at different growth phases, all the members of the team contribute important input at every stage. Regular comprehensive evaluations and subsequent treatment by experts ensures the best possible outcome for every facet of the cleft condition.

Such teams can be found in almost every metropolitan area, as well as in many areas that may be considered less metropolitan. How does one go about finding such a team, and who are the specialists that may be working with the cleft-affected child? Can you hope for good treatment and repair without a team? These are good questions.

First, good treatment CAN be accomplished without the services of a team per se, but the chances are great that BETTER treatment can be assured in a team setting. Many people live long distances from the nearest craniofacial team center and it is not practical to travel the distance for treatment. However, annual or semi-annual evaluations by a team may provide valuable suggestions to the physician who is actually working with the child. Also, whether or not the child has work that is done by an actual recognized team, there remains a team of professionals working with the child (you may have a pediatrician, a plastic surgeon, an orthodontist, and ENT, etc.,) In such a case it is important that those professionals work well together and regularly consult concerning the child whose treatment they share. While there may be, and always are exceptions, the basic rule is that the care of a child with a cleft will be most comprehensive if provided by a craniofacial or cleft palate team.

Most families find the team in their area through a referral by their obstetrician or pediatrician. Some insurance carriers actually require that you obtain the services of an area team before they will provide coverage, and therefore make a referral. If you are not aware of any cleft palate team in your area you can call the Cleft Palate Foundation at 1-800-24-CLEFT. They will let you know of any teams practicing near you.

Who makes up their craniofacial team? They may not all be doctors. They are a collection of medical and social service providers who speak to the needs of the child born with a cleft and that child's family. The following persons may or may not be on the team treating your child. If one discipline is missing from your team and you feel your child is in need of services provided by that field, your team could refer you to someone in your area.

SURGEON

The Surgeon is often considered the "Captain" of the team. This person provides the plastic, reconstructive surgery on the cleft. This person will close the lip and the palate and provide for any scar revision and rhinoplasty. The plastic surgery to repair and reconstruct the cleft is often done by a Plastic Surgeon. Other persons who may do the plastic surgery include Oral Maxillofacial surgeons, Otolaryngologists, etc. What is important is that the surgeon you choose have experience with and a commitment to cleft repair.

PEDIATRICIAN

The pediatrician looks at the overall well-being of the child. The pediatrician checks the normal growth and development of the child and makes certain that the child is physically fit for upcoming surgical procedures.

PEDIATRIC DENTIST

The role of the pediatric dentist is to ensure that the child's teeth are healthy and strong. Many times children with clefts have teeth in unlikely positions in the mouth. It is sometimes very difficult to keep those teeth clean and therefore healthy. The pediatric dentist helps to maintain a healthy and cavity-free mouth.

ORTHODONTIST

The orthodontist, on the other hand, helps to establish a good shape to the dental arches. A child with cleft may need the services of an orthodontist even before she has teeth! The orthodontist will work to achieve a normal dental arch prior to bone graft surgery, and then follow-up to maintain the integrity of that arch once achieved. The orthodontist will be an active participant in much of the cleft-affected child's care.

PROSTHODONTIST

There are times when a child with a cleft needs a prosthetic device to meet her specific needs. Such prosthetic devices may be an obturator, a bridge, a retainer, an implant, or any one of a number of other devices. The prosthodontist works very closely with the orthodontist and the surgeon to provide the cleft-affected child with necessary appliances.

OTOLARYNGOLOGIST

Sometimes called an ENT (Ear Nose & Throat Doctor), the Otolaryngologist helps to keep the ears functioning and clear. Children with clefts typically suffer from poorly functioning Eustachian Tubes and therefore experience a larger than normal number of ear infections. The Otolaryngologist serves to keep those infections at a minimum, and to minimize any damage done subsequent to such infections.

AUDIOLOGIST

The audiologist checks the child's hearing regularly. Recurring ear infections, waxy build-up and fluid behind the eardrum (all common among children with clefts) can rob a child of the ability to hear effectively. The Audiologist measures how well a child is hearing and makes recommendations if a child's hearing is compromised.

SPEECH AND LANGUAGE PATHOLOGIST

The Speech and Language Pathologist assists the child in producing intelligible language. The Speech and Language Pathologist will provide therapy in areas of articulation and language development, depending upon the child's unique need. It may be likely, due to the nature of speech therapy, that your child may see more of the Speech and Language Pathologist, and on a more regular basis, than any other member of the team.

COMMUNITY HEALTH NURSE

The Community Health Nurse assesses the health needs of the entire family and makes recommendations concerning resources that might aid in maintaining the overall health of the household. The Community Health Nurse may also help by instructing the parents on how to feed and otherwise care for the child.

GENETICIST

The Geneticist studies various aspects of the family, the family history, etc. and assists the family in determining a recurrence risk when choosing whether or not to have more children. The Geneticist helps the family gain an understanding concerning the factors that contribute to clefting conditions. The geneticist will also help persons of childbearing age who were born with clefts to determine the probability of producing a cleft-affected child themselves. A geneticist will also look for potential syndromes that may be at the root of the cleft.

CLINICAL SOCIAL WORKER

The Clinical Social Worker helps the family to deal with all the issues that touch them concerning the cleft. Issues of grief, finance, emotional and moral support, feelings of anger and guilt, and so forth, are non-medical topics that affect the over-all treatment of the child and the family. The Clinical Social Worker will help the family to access appropriate resources and to network for support.

PSYCHOLOGIST

The Psychologist works with the child alone, the parents alone, or the family as a group to ensure normal functioning. Many times parents find a child's disability or deformity difficult to adjust to. Oftentimes a child with a cleft has self-esteem issues that limit his potential. The Psychologist will provide intervention that speaks directly to those needs.

The child born with a cleft presents a large package of treatment concerns. The particulars of that package are diverse. The craniofacial team is by definition a group of experts capable of speaking to each of the issues that child might present.

How often a child visits the team depends on many factors. Those factors include the child's age and stage of reconstruction; distance between the clinic and the child's home; the specific needs presented by the child at that point in time; the requirements of the insurance carrier; and many more. But because the craniofacial team provides experts in all the disciplines that affect a child with a cleft lip and palate, team treatment and evaluation is most highly recommended.

GETTING THROUGH THE TWO-HOUR TOUGH

The morning of surgery has arrived. You've prepared. You've packed. And you've readied yourself for the ordeal. You've entrusted your child into the hands of the medical profession and the big double doors of the surgical unit have closed between you and your precious baby. Thus begins the two toughest hours of a parent's life - the time of the actual surgery.

Just before surgery is not the worst. You certainly have the nerve-wracking anticipation of all that your child will endure. You have your dreaded imagination to contend with. But it is not the worst. Before the surgery you can prepare yourself and your child. Before the surgery you have some control.

Just after the surgery is not the worst. Your child will be sick from anesthesia and in pain. There will be feeding issues and aftercare. But it is not the worst. After the surgery you can hold your child and give her comfort. You can follow the aftercare regimen to enhance the healing process. After the surgery you have some control.

But during the surgery - THAT'S the worst. During the surgery you have little or no control. You cannot touch your child with reassurance. You cannot watch the doctor to make certain everything is being done with the utmost of care and concern for your child's well being. You are on one side of the big doors and your child is a world away on the other side of those doors. And all you can do is wait and watch the clock.

Actually, the best thing you can do during your child's surgery is get through it with the least amount of anxiety possible. I know how difficult that is to do. I am a mother and I have spent my share of hours in the little room waiting. But there are some tricks to making the time pass quickly until you can be reunited with your child and the healing begins.

First, if possible, don't spend the entire time in the waiting room. Of course, if your child is having a procedure that takes very little time, stick around. But if the surgery is expected to take more than an hour, try not to spend the whole time in the waiting room. HOWEVER, by the same token do NOT make yourself unavailable! The nurse or the Candy Striper should know where you can be reached if you leave the waiting area. Some hospitals equip parents with beepers that they can carry with them to other areas of the hospital so that they can be beeped as soon as they are needed. If your hospital does not offer that valuable option, you may want to suggest it to them.

Most children are scheduled for morning surgery and must arrive at the hospital fasting. Therefore, most parents have also not eaten breakfast before surgery (who would want to eat in front of a hungry child?) It may be a healthy idea to plan to have breakfast in the hospital cafeteria right after the surgery begins. Not only will it help the time to pass, but you will be energized and ready to be there for your child when she really needs you.

You may want to take a walk to the hospital gift shop. It may make you feel closer to your child if you pick out a book or a toy or a colorful balloon to share in the room after the surgery is over. (Realistically, your child will most likely not be interested in those gifts right away after surgery, but by the second day she will.)

When we are anxious about something we produce a lot of adrenaline. Unfortunately, in the hospital setting, while we are waiting for our child to reappear there are few opportunities to release that adrenaline. If you feel you have the time, take a brisk walk outside or through the halls of the hospital. Always make sure you are back in the waiting area at least a half hour before you expect the surgery to be over.

If you are like me, however, you probably feel uncomfortable leaving the waiting area at all. In that case, try not to wait alone. If your spouse cannot be with you, perhaps your mother or a close friend or minister can come and wait with you. Good conversation is often very comforting and helps to pass the time. Also, many hospitals allow parents to go into the recovery room after surgery and help to comfort the child. If you are asked to go to recovery, it would be nice if there were someone you could trust to leave your personal belongings with (your purse, coat, reading material, etc.) until your child moves to her room.

Some parents try to spend the waiting time reading. I find that I am much too distracted to get any serious reading done. However, others find the distraction to be incredibly liberating. Even if you are not able to read with your heart in your throat, you will still want reading material. There will be long spells of nothing to do but watch the baby sleep after the surgery is over.

Other parents prefer to write. Some keep journal accounts of their hospital experiences. Others spend this time writing a letter to the baby that will go into the baby book and be shared in years to come. Not only is that a cathartic exercise that will help to relieve the stress, but it also can prove to be interesting and helpful to your child when she is older.

Regardless of what you do, the time will eventually pass. It is when the surgery is over that you will be needed. It is after the surgery that you can help your child to heal. During the surgery, your job is to get through it. Remind yourself that your child is in capable hands. Your child is asleep and in no pain. And the procedure is necessary for the health and normal function of your child.

And if you still worry, take heart. You are just being a normal parent. But don't let the natural worry that you feel make you an ineffective parent. You help your child most by getting through the anxiety and being there for her when the surgery is done.

Finally, never, ever forget – what you do today, you do FOR your child, and not TO her. It's a very important difference.

Gallery of Hope

Just Look at Us Now!

Jacob was born with a unilateral cleft lip and palate and an incredibly wide smile!

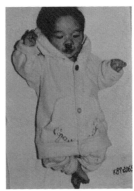

Joey had a very wide bilateral cleft.

At three years of age, Jacob (on the left) and Joey are a couple of handsome dudes!

At age 18, look at them now! Joey, on the right, and brother, Jacob – Handsome and happy, accomplished scholars and ready to meet the world.

Jacob and Joey

JESSICA

Born in Korea with a bilateral cleft lip and palate, this is the picture that referred her for

When her adoption was finalized at two years of age, this little charmer was well on her way to becoming an American Beauty!

At fourteen, Jessica enjoys all the privileges of teen-hood.

Chris was born with a unilateral
cleft lip and palate.

At age 13, Chris is quite the young man!

CHRISTOPHER

What a serious 3 year old!

&

HAILEY

At Three months old, Hailey is all smiles!

Hailey's a cute little ducky at
seven months old.

Hailey, 5, and big sister, Tiffany, 12.

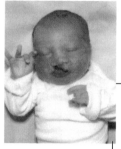

Precious Zach and a unilateral cleft.

12 years old, and he must be a good kid. Big sister, Kristi still loves him!

ZACHARY

&

What a smile!

RACHEL

At age 10 1/2, Rachel is a natural beauty

Sleeping baby Rachel, she has a bilateral cleft.

Surgery closed the cleft for her

Well, hello, little one. Sheldon has a bilateral cleft lip.

After lip repair surgery, look who's all smiles!

SHELDON

&

ASHLIE

Aloha, Mr. Handsome, Dude. Sheldon, at age 10.

Lip and palate, both repaired, at age 12 months, this girl's got places to go!

Also with a bilateral cleft, Ashlie is such a sweet baby.

At age 6, Ashlie is such a beauty. Was there ever any doubt?

Newborn Laura

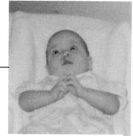

Sweet baby, 3 months old

LAURA

Laura is sweet sixteen!

&

LEVI

Sweet baby Levi, such a precious boy!

A happy little guy at age four.

Did Santa give him a tongue for Christmas?

LARA

Lara is the 4 year old queen of the playground set!

All smiles and a bilateral cleft lip and palate, Lara's smile could melt a heart!

At 12 years old, Lara's beauty is Undeniable .

A VERY SPECIAL THANKS TO ALL THE CHILDREN AND FAMILIES WHO HAVE SO GRACIOUSLY SHARED THEIR PHOTOS AND THEIR LIVES IN THIS GALLERY, OFFERING HOPE AND HEALING TO OTHER NEW FAMILIES.

*** BE NOT AFRAID, YOUNG MOTHER ***

Be not afraid, young mother,
And do not feel so all alone.
There are others who've traveled the road you now walk.
We'll gladly help guide you along.

Be not disheartened, young mother,
For days of unknowns full of dread.
For though there be trials And challenges,
There also lies joy up ahead.

Be not discouraged, young mother.
We know of your loss, pain and fear.
But behind that dark cloud looms a rainbow of love
That will shine for you year after year.

Be touched by your joy, young mother.
For that beautiful baby, your own!
And no matter the challenges that may lie ahead,
Neither you nor your child are alone.

NATIONAL RESOURCES OF INTEREST
TO FAMILIES OF CRANIOFACIALLY-AFFECTED
CHILDREN

Wide Smiles:
Offers support and information for families dealing with cleft or other craniofacial issues. The website at www.widesmiles.org contains hundreds of documents on information about cleft issues in the cleftlinks section. A gallery of over 100 cleft affected persons have shared their before and after surgical pictures. The children's literature section offers children's stories, including a puppet script, that can be shared in public schools. There are many other pages and lots more information, all free!

Cleft-Talk
Offers a forum in which parents offer help to parents and they can all discuss topics that only another parent of a cleft-affected child can understand. Daily discussions on anything and everything related to life with a cleft. Subscribe and you'll receive messages via email every day. You choose whether to respond or not... but still gain insight and share others' experiences. Cleft-Talk Subscription instructions: send email to: majordomo@bmtmicro.com subject: no subject -- body of message: subscribe cleft_talk2

Cleft Palate Foundation
Provides information concerning location of craniofacial teams, support groups, other resources, as well as various literature. 1-800-24-CLEFT

Craniofacial Foundation of America FACES
Provides free newsletter and produces other educaional materials and networks for families. Offers financial support for nonmedical expenses related to treatment.

Lynne Mayfield, Director
P.O. Box 11082, Chattanooga, TN 37401
(423) 266-1632 or (800) 332-2373
E-mail: faces@faces-cranio.org
Web: http://www.faces-cranio.org

Other Books by Author,
Joanne Green

Hootah's Baby

Most children have happy, untroubled childhoods. But not all. There are some who are placed in harm's way, if even temporarily, by their own parents' lack of parental skills. When that happens, often, the courts must step in, in the best interests of the child. But when that happens, it is the child who often does not understand the dynamics of this very complicated situation.

Hootah's Baby is an allegorical story about a mother owl whose life-style choices have made it impossible to be an effective mother. The community steps in to ensure the baby's safety. It is not about whether or not the mother loves her baby. It is all about mothering skills and the child's need to be safe.

Hootah's Baby is a tool to be used to help children of court-ordered relinquishment and/or state custody to understand the complex issues that have led to their current life situation. Helps are included for the adult who reads this book with these children to be able to assist them to open windows of communication that will help them understand basic truths: they are not at fault; the courts are not the bad guys; and their mothers do, in fact, love them.

To My Child, Concerning Your Birthmother

Children of adoption are wanted, loved, cherished, and in a sense, chosen. Yet, even in the midst of all that love, the questions sometimes nag at the heart of the adopted child, "Didn't my birthmother love me? How could she give me away?"

In truth, an adoption choice is one of the hardest, most heart-breaking, most selfless choices a birthmother can ever make. Whether born of fear, confusion, or even desperation, it is never arrived at easily. It is a sacrificial decision based on what is best for this child she so deeply loves.

This book is written to help children of adoption to understand what may have been behind those first circumstances in their lives, and to answer the question, "Why did my birthmother choose adoption for me?"

To purchase these books, order at www.sagabooks.net

About the Author

Joanne Green spent sixteen years actively failing at her goal of becoming a mother. After a long, frustrating and often painful road, she was offered a tiny premature boy in Korea. He was born with a cleft lip and palate. Joanne said, "YES!!!" Seventy-two days later, her world changed forever as she welcomed Jacob home.

Eventually, Joanne would adopt two more times – and both times, the child was born with a cleft. "It's not that I asked the agency for cleft-affected children," she explains. "I didn't. It's just that these are the children that were meant to be mine, and the cleft was not enough to make me consider saying no."

Shortly after the adoptions of her sons, Joanne founded Wide Smiles, a support and information network for families of children born with cleft lip and palate. Wide Smiles quickly grew to have an international influence and soon went onto the World Wide Web (www.widesmiles.org). She also founded Cleft Talk, an online email-driven support group of families and individuals who are affected by cleft or other craniofacial challenges. Membership in Cleft talk has spanned the world, once boasting of having parents on every continent in the world (Yes, even Antarctica – for a short time, anyway!)

Joanne graduated from the University of the Pacific with a degree in Psychology. She now lives in Stockton, California with her family, where she teaches sixth grade in the public schools while she also continues to function as the director of Wide Smiles. In her spare time, she writes.

Families wishing to join Cleft talk may do so at no charge.

Send an email to majordomo@bmtmicro.com
Leave the subject field blank, or state no subject.
In the message field, type in "Subscribe cleft_talk2"

We invite you to peruse the Wide Smiles website at
www.widesmiles.org

About the Illustrator

Marla Verdone prayed for a special baby and God answered that prayer by sending Lara Rose into her life. Lara was born with a bilateral cleft lip and palate. There was not a lot of support or information available for new parents of cleft affected babies in her area until she made some connections months later. She then decided to hook up and share support and resources to other new parents of cleft babies at area hospitals. The biggest of these resources that she proudly shares with them is Wide Smiles. She is an advocate for many children's issues: Cleft related, health insurance, dyslexia and education to name a few.

Marla holds a BFA from the Art Institute of Boston. She likes to keep her life flexible so substitute teaches public school and is self employed as an Independent Pampered Chef Consultant and Freelance Artist.

She is a proud military wife and lives in Janesville, Wisconsin with her family. When time allows she likes to perform music with all her Fife and Drum Corps friends and create art and bake. Her favorite is spending time with family serving as #1 fan to daughters Lara and Lexandra who truly inspire her.

Also from SagaBooks….

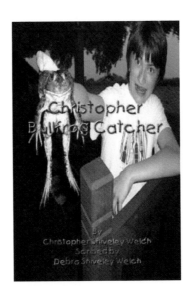

CHRISTOPHER BULLFROG CATCHER

By Christopher Shiveley Welch , scribed by Debra Shiveley Welch

This young author, Christopher, was born with a complete unilateral cleft lip and palate.

Christopher's mother, Debra, has been a member of Wide Smiles (**www.widesmiles.org**)
and Cleft Talk, the Wide Smiles email-based support network, since Christopher was four-years old.

Debra is also the Fundraising Coordinator for Wide Smiles.

Christopher Bullfrog Catcher, **as well as other titles by Joanne Greene, can be found at www.sagabooks.net**

CPSIA information can be obtained
at www.ICGtesting.com
Printed in the USA
LVIC04n2237130315
430543LV00008B/42